THE ADVENTURES OF THE DISH AND THE SPOON

Hey Diddle Diddle

The Cat and the fiddle

The Cow jumped over the moon

The little Dog laughed to see such fun

MINI GREY

ALFRED A. KNOPF  NEW YORK

Someone
put a record
on the new
record player.

It was playing
our tune.

How could we resist?

The Dish whirled around
on the moonlit ocean.

I didn't know
where we were going,
and I didn't care.

I knew the Dish
would take us there.

We tried our luck as an act in a vaudeville show.

The audience loved us!

We were famous.

RITZY

THE DISH
THE & SPOON

The Dish got a taste for the high life.
We bought a motor car.
The Dish shopped for
jewelry and furs.

Soon our money
was
all
gone.

A gang
of sharp
and shady
characters
offered to
lend us some.

They tried to frighten the Dish.

What could we do?

We couldn't pay them back.

"Stop!
Untie the Dish!"
I screamed.
"I've got a plan!"

"No one will recognize us,"
    I whispered.
"Just march into the bank
    and it'll be over in
no time."

WANTED

Have you seen these two dangerous criminals?
Wanted for unarmed robbery at the City Bank
Generous reward for their capture
Contact the Police Department with information

Oh, we were so foolish!
Of course they recognized us.
We'd appeared on posters all
over the country.

We tried using
    some of our old tricks
        for our getaway . . .

. . . but we didn't see
that sharp rock
sticking out.

"Run while you can, Spoon," breathed the Dish.

But the Dish
was broken
and so was I.

I let them
lock me up
and turned away
from the moon.

Twenty-five years later,
I'd done my time.

I blinked in the sunny street.
The world had really changed.

What home could there be
for a lonely, broken old
spoon like me?

Then I saw this shop.
"Perfect," I said.

I heard a soft sobbing.
Those faded flowers
looked familiar.

rgains
alore!
ll under
wo pennies

"Dish?" I whispered.
"Is that you?"
"Don't look at me, Spoon,"
she wept. "I am old and cracked,
and my glaze is crazed."

"Dish," I said, "you look just
the same as you did the
June night we ran away."

The Dish sniffed.

Someone had put
a record on the old
gramophone player.

The sound was scratchy,
but we knew that tune.

"Can you remember the old tricks, Dish?"
I asked. The Dish nodded.
"Well, there's a whole new world out there.
People who have
never seen dishes
do tricks with
spoons."

THE DISH AND THE SPOON

Every

Night

Admission
FREE

THIS IS A BORZOI BOOK
PUBLISHED BY ALFRED A. KNOPF

Published in the United States by Alfred A. Knopf, an imprint of Random House Children's Books, a division of Random House, Inc., New York and simultaneously in Canada by Random House of Canada Limited, Toronto. Published in Great Britain in 2006 by Jonathan Cape, an imprint of Random House Children's Books.
First American edition, May 2006.

www.randomhouse.com/kids

To the one and only PiPPA

Educators and librarians, for a variety of teaching tools, visit us at www.randomhouse.com/teachers

Library of Congress Cataloging-in-Publication Data available upon request
ISBN 0-375-83691-8 (trade) / ISBN 0-375-93691-2 (lib. bdg.)
ISBN 0-375-83691-8 (trade) · 10 9 8 7 6 5 4 3 2

MANUFACTURED IN MALAYSIA

First American Edition